The Blueberry Cake
That Little Fox Baked

The Blueberry Cake That Little Fox Baked

written & illustrated by
Andrea Da Rif

A Margaret K. McElderry Book

Atheneum   1984   New York

Library of Congress Cataloging in Publication Data
Da Rif, Andrea.
The blueberry cake that little fox baked.
"A Margaret K. McElderry book."
Summary: Mistakenly believing that it is his
mother's birthday, Little Fox goes to
a lot of trouble to bake a special cake.
[1. Foxes—Fiction.   2. Cake—Fiction]   I. Title.
PZ7.D244Bl 1984   [E]   84-444
ISBN 0-689-50307-5

Published simultaneously in Canada by McClelland & Stewart, Ltd.
Composition by Dix Type Inc., Syracuse, New York
Printed by Connecticut Printers
Bound by Halliday Lithograph Corporation
First Edition

To my mother,
with thanks for all your love
and encouragement
and to Kev, for the same.

Little Fox was feeling lazy. His father and mother and sister and brother were already having breakfast. He could hear them laughing and talking. But he was still in bed and it felt so snug he didn't want to get up.

Then his father called to him. "We're leaving, Little Fox. We've let you have a good long sleep, but now you must get up. Remember not to be late. We'll see you there." Then the door slammed and the house was quiet.

What was happening today that he shouldn't be late for, Little Fox wondered. He stretched, climbed lazily out of bed and went to look at the calendar.

Today was circled in red. That meant something important. Underneath the date—written in neat, small letters—it said "B.Day." It must be somebody's birthday. It wasn't *his* birthday. He kn▪ that. The leaves on the trees were always turning red and gold on his birthday.

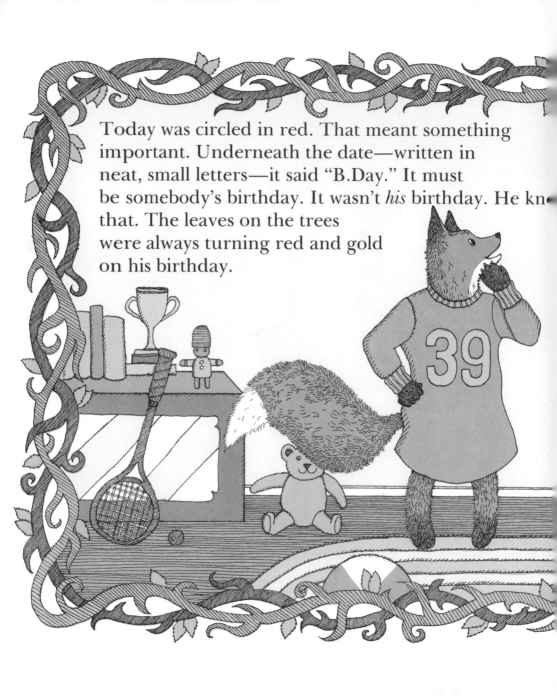

S	M	T	W	T	F	S
		1	2	3	4	5
6	7	8	9	10	11	12
13	14	15	16	17	18	19
20	21	22	23	24	25	26
27	28	29	30			

It wasn't his sister's or his brother's birthday. There was always snow on the ground on their birthdays. It must be his mother's birthday. Of course! His whole family would be going to Grandmother's for a party. He *mustn't* be late.

Little Fox wanted to do something very, very special for his mother to show her how much he loved her. He thought hard for a few minutes.

It was blueberry time and the berries were at
their sweetest and ripest right now. He
decided to bake his mother a blueberry cake.
Then he could take it to Grandmother's.

First he had to pick the berries, and he knew
just the place to go.

The best ones were at the top of the bush so he tried to climb up.

He tried again.

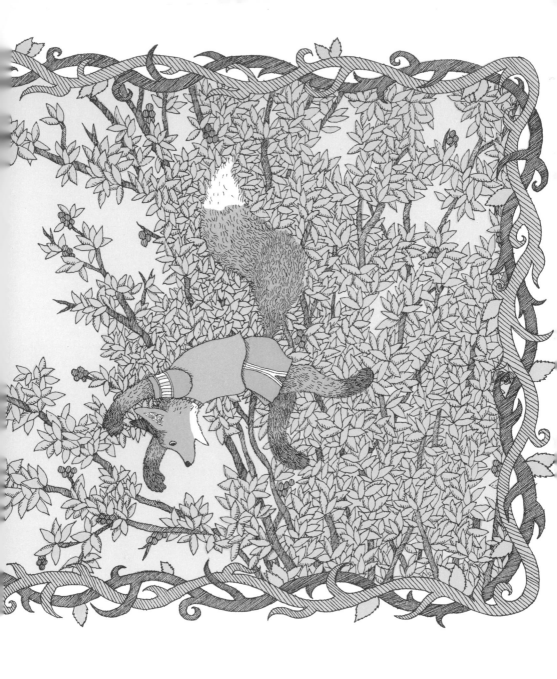

At last the great hawk helped him.

Little Fox took the berries back to the
kitchen. Then he gathered up all the things
he needed for his cake. A few other things
fell down, but he could pick them up later.

Milk, flour, honey, and two eggs went into the mixing bowl. He stirred very hard. Next he added the berries. The bowl was a little small and some of the batter spilled. But it looked delicious!

When the oven was good and hot, Little Fox
poured the batter into a pan and carefully
put it in the oven to bake. Then he sat down
to wait.

Suddenly the door opened with a bang! His father and mother and sister and brother stormed in. They looked very angry.

"Little Fox," said his father sternly. "We have been waiting and waiting for you. Today is Blueberry Day, the day of the big blueberry festival, and everyone is there except you! I told you this morning not to be late."

"Little Fox," added his mother. "Look at yourself! Look at this kitchen! What a mess! Just what have you been up to? Whatever it is, you have been very thoughtless today."

Little Fox began to cry. So "B.Day" had not meant "Birthday." It had meant "Blueberry Day." Through his tears he explained what had happened.

For a moment there was silence.
Then his mother hugged him.
His father patted him on the
back. His sister and brother
smiled at him.

"The festival isn't over yet," said his father. "We came to look for you while they get ready to serve lunch. Now *you* can bring the most special dessert of all!" Little Fox felt very happy. "You hurry to the festival," said his mother with a big smile. "Your father and I will wait here until the cake is done."